Rabén & Sjögren Bokförlag, Stockholm
http://www.raben.se

Translation copyright © 1998 by Rabén & Sjögren Bokförlag
All rights reserved
Originally published in Sweden by Eriksson & Lindgren under
the title *Tick-Tack*, pictures and text copyright © 1996 by Lena Anderson.
Library of Congress catalog card number: 97-69293
Printed in Italy
First edition, 1998

ISBN 91 29 64074 1

Lena Anderson

TICK-TOCK

R&S
BOOKS

Stockholm   New York   London   Adelaide   Toronto

1

Tick-tock, it's one o'clock.
Who wants to go to the park with Will?

2

Tick-tock, it's two o'clock.
Who wants to climb the old oak tree?

3

Tick-tock, it's three o'clock.
When Hedgehog falls, we've all had enough.

Tick-tock, it's four o'clock.
Who wants a piece of sunshine cake?

5

Tick-tock, it's five o'clock.
Come on, everybody, we're going home!

6

Tick-tock, it's six o'clock.
Put on your p.j.'s and get a big hug.

Tick-tock, it's seven o'clock.
Let's brush our teeth and go to bed.

Tick-tock, it's eight o'clock.
Duck wakes up and needs his potty.

Tick-tock, it's nine o'clock.
Little Elephant's had a bad dream.

10

Tick-tock, it's ten o'clock.
Who's awake now? It's a wild little Pig.

11

Tick-tock, it's eleven o'clock.
Hedgehog must have a drink of water.

12

Tick-tock, it's twelve o'clock.
Will's asleep and the story's over.